# Polar Bear Puzzle

# Adventures of Riley™

# Polar Bear Puzzle

BY

**Amanda Lumry**

AND

**Laura Hurwitz**

Dear Riley,

We're worried about polar bears, the Arctic's largest predators! Every year they're becoming skinnier and weaker, and giving birth to fewer cubs, and scientists aren't sure why. Aunt Martha, Cousin Alice, and I are going to the Arctic town of Churchill, Canada, to get to the bottom of this mystery. What do you say, Riley— will you "bear" with us?

Uncle Max

SCHOLASTIC INC.

New York • Toronto • London • Auckland • Sydney
Mexico City • New Delhi • Hong Kong • Buenos Aires

First published in China in 2007 by Eaglemont Press.
www.eaglemont.com

All photographs by Amanda Lumry except:
Page 25 caribou herd © Joseph Van Os/Getty Images
Page 25 caribou © Paul Nicklen/Getty Images
Pages 26–27 polar bears on ice © Johnny Johnson/Getty Images
Page 32 global warming map by NASA
Page 33 "Definitions of the Arctic" map by UNEP/GRID-Arendal Maps and
Graphics Library. 2005. UNEP/GRID-Arendal. 12 Jul 2007
http://maps.grida.no/go/graphic/definitions_of_the_arctic

Illustrations and Layouts by Ulkutay & Ulkutay, London WC2E 9RZ
Editing and Digital Compositing by Michael E. Penman
Digital Imaging by Phoenix Color

Library of Congress Control Number: 2007017589

ISBN-13: 978-0-545-06838-3
ISBN-10: 0-545-06838-X

10 9 8 7 6 5 4 3 2 1                    09 10 11 12 13

Printed in the U.S.A.        08
First Scholastic paperback printing, January 2009

FSC

**Mixed Sources**
Product group from well-managed
forests, controlled sources and
recycled wood or fiber

Cert no. SGS-COC-003338
www.fsc.org
© 1996 Forest Stewardship Council

A portion of the proceeds from your purchase of this licensed product
supports the stated educational mission of the Smithsonian Institution—
"the increase and diffusion of knowledge." The name of the
Smithsonian Institution and the sunburst logo are registered trademarks
of the Smithsonian Institution and are registered in the U.S. Patent and
Trademark Office. www.si.edu

2% of the proceeds from this book will be donated to the Wildlife
Conservation Society. http://wcs.org

An average royalty of approximately 3 cents from the sale of each book
in the Adventures of Riley series will be received by World Wildlife Fund
(WWF) to support their international efforts to protect endangered species
and their habitats. ® WWF Registered Trademark Panda Symbol ©
1986 WWF. © 1986 Panda symbol WWF–World Wide Fund For Nature
(also known as World Wildlife Fund) ® "WWF" is a WWF Registered
Trademark © 1986 WWF–Fonds Mondial pour la Nature symbole du panda
Marque Déposée du WWF ®
www.worldwildlife.org

We try to produce the most beautiful books possible and we are extremely
concerned about the impact of our manufacturing process on the forests of
the world and the environment as a whole. Accordingly, we made sure that
the paper used in this book has been certified as coming from forests that
are managed to ensure the protection of the people and wildlife dependent
upon them.

**Riley was so excited!** His class was visiting the new polar bear exhibit at the zoo.

"Polar bears are huge!" Riley told his friend Mike. "And look how much they eat!"

"A well-fed bear is a happy bear," said the zookeeper, as she tossed fish after fish to the hungry bears.

I'll have to remember that, thought Riley.

A few weeks later, in early November, Riley took a jet to Winnipeg, Canada, and then a smaller plane to Churchill. He stepped off the plane into a swirling sea of white.

Inside the airport, Alice and Aunt Martha both said, "Welcome to the polar bear capital of the world!"

"But be careful!" said Uncle Max. "There are a lot of hungry polar bears wandering around town, looking for food. They've been waiting since the spring thaw for Hudson Bay to freeze over again, so they can return to the ice pack to hunt for seals. The bay is usually frozen by now, so the bears are restless. Just yesterday, we had to put three of them in jail."

"Jail?" asked Riley.

"The 'jail' is a pen where we keep polar bears that have broken into houses or garbage cans searching for food," said Aunt Martha. "We give them checkups, tag them, and then use a helicopter to drop them back into the wild. By giving checkups to as many bears as possible, we hope to find out what is causing their population to get smaller and weaker."

"Isn't that dangerous?" asked Riley, getting into the bus.

"It's okay," said Alice. "The bears are sound asleep when they're tagged."

Later, they switched from their bus to a **tundra buggy** so they could tag polar bears on the way to their Hudson Bay hotel.

Before long, Riley spotted a black nose in the snow.

"Uncle Max! Look!" Riley shouted. Suddenly, the black nose vanished. "Hey, wait, where'd it go?"

"The bear covered his nose with his paw and now we can't see him!" said Aunt Martha. "Local stories say they do this to blend into the snow better."

"I'll drive closer so I can shoot him," Uncle Max said.

"Shoot?" Riley cried. Uncle Max smiled.

"Don't worry, I'm only using a **tranquilizer** dart. It won't hurt him, and since the medicine in the dart puts him to sleep, he won't hurt us, either. Are you ready for your first patient, Riley?"

Before Riley could answer, Uncle Max's dart hit the bear in the shoulder, and the bear went down in a heap.

## Tundra

➤ The tundra is a vast, flat, frozen desert found in the polar regions.

➤ The word tundra means "tree-less" in Finnish.

➤ Below the surface is a layer of soil called perma-frost, which stays frozen permanently!

—Maxwell "Uncle Max" Plimpton, Professor and Senior Field Biologist

# Polar Bear Tagging

## Measuring

➤ Using a tape measure, the length and width of the bear are carefully measured and recorded.

➤ The bear is also weighed with a large, heavy-duty scale.

➤ Yearly measurements are used to see if the bear is staying healthy and getting enough to eat.

## Scientific Samples

➤ Blood, fat, hair, and tissue samples provide valuable information about the bear's health (what it's eating, if it's stored up enough fat for the summer, and if it has any diseases).

➤ A small, unneeded tooth is pulled out so it can be viewed under a microscope. The age of the bear can be found by counting the layers of **cementum** in the tooth.

## RFID Tagging

➤ A long-range RFID (Radio Frequency Identification) tag is attached to the bear's ear.

➤ With RFID, tagged bears can be identified from a plane or helicopter flying as high as 1,800 ft. (549 m) above the Arctic ice.

➤ This lets scientists learn about the bear's habits, diet, and behaviors quickly and safely.

8

"Alice, are there any other bears around?" asked Uncle Max. She shook her head. "Great. Let's get to work."

"Are you sure this is safe?" Riley asked.

"Positive," said Uncle Max, taking out his tools. With Riley's help, the checkup took less than an hour.

"That's it!" said Aunt Martha. "Now let's get back into the **tundra buggy** before he wakes up!"

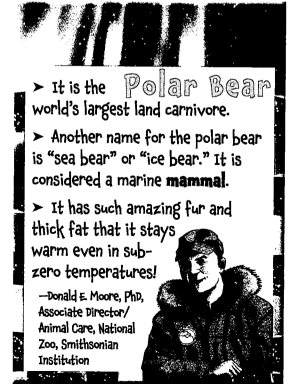

➤ It is the **Polar Bear** world's largest land carnivore.

➤ Another name for the polar bear is "sea bear" or "ice bear." It is considered a marine **mammal**.

➤ It has such amazing fur and thick fat that it stays warm even in sub-zero temperatures!

—Donald E. Moore, PhD, Associate Director/ Animal Care, National Zoo, Smithsonian Institution

After tagging a few more bears, they arrived at their hotel—a **stationary** "train" made up of connected **tundra buggies**. There were sleeping cars, viewing cars, and even a dining car.

"Why do polar bears need the ice to catch seals?" Riley asked at dinner.

"Although polar bears are great swimmers, they are slow and clumsy hunters in the open water," said Aunt Martha.

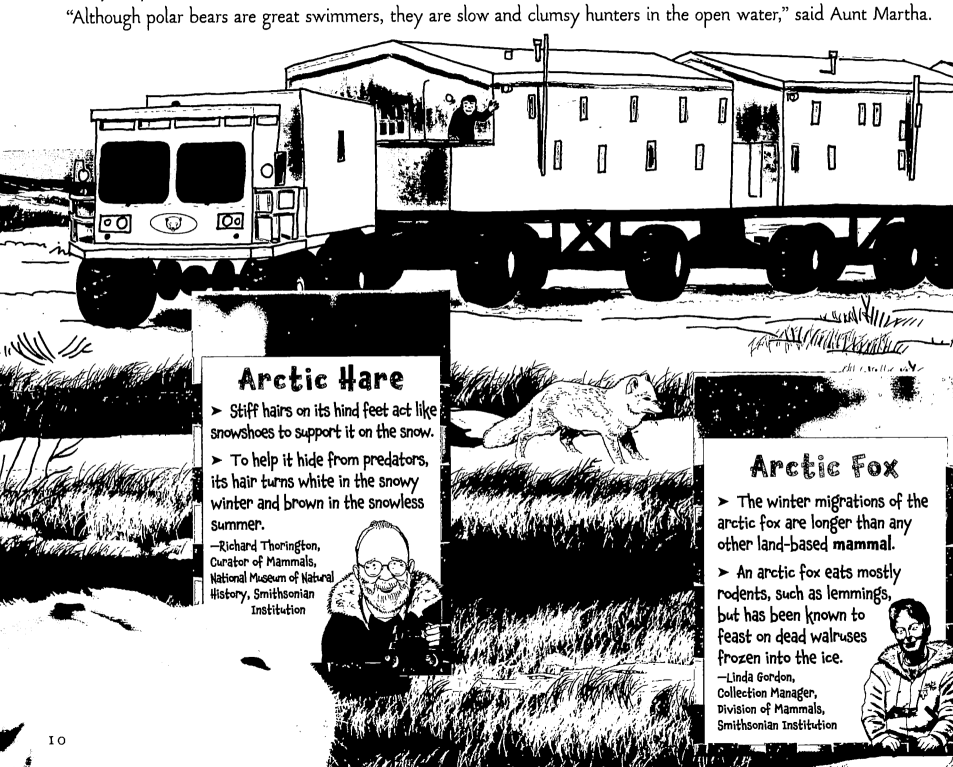

## Arctic Hare

➤ Stiff hairs on its hind feet act like snowshoes to support it on the snow.

➤ To help it hide from predators, its hair turns white in the snowy winter and brown in the snowless summer.

—Richard Thorington,
Curator of Mammals,
National Museum of Natural
History, Smithsonian
Institution

## Arctic Fox

➤ The winter migrations of the arctic fox are longer than any other land-based **mammal**.

➤ An arctic fox eats mostly rodents, such as lemmings, but has been known to feast on dead walruses frozen into the ice.

—Linda Gordon,
Collection Manager,
Division of Mammals,
Smithsonian Institution

"They prefer to hunt from the ice, waiting patiently by air holes for seals to come up to breathe. Then the polar bears use their big paws and sharp claws to snatch the seals from the water," said Uncle Max.

I'm glad I'm not a seal, thought Riley.

## Snowy Owl

➤ It spends most of its time **perched** still and silent, looking and listening for prey.

➤ Pairs of snowy owls will defend their nest against all predators, even wolves!

—Carter Roberts, President and CEO, World Wildlife Fund

The night grew bright as magical green and white lights began dancing across the sky.

"Riley, it's the northern lights!" cried Alice. They both watched in wonder.

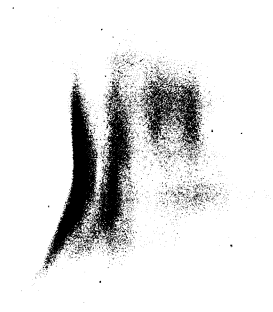

## Northern Lights

➤ The northern lights (scientific name: *aurora borealis*) happen when tiny particles from the sun **collide** with gases in Earth's **atmosphere**.

➤ The lights occur most often in late fall and early spring.

➤ While visible on most clear nights in the Arctic, they are seen only every 200 years at the equator.

—David Aguilar, Director, Science and Public Programming, Harvard-Smithsonian Center for Astrophysics

In the morning, they took a **tundra buggy** back to Churchill. Hudson Bay still hadn't frozen over, and the polar bears were getting even hungrier.

## Ptarmigan

➤ It will burrow under the snow to keep warm.

➤ Its feathers are snow-white in winter and brown, gray, and white in summer.

➤ Its legs and toes are covered with feathers to keep its feet warm.

—Randy Snodgrass, Director, Government Relations, World Wildlife Fund

That night, in his new hotel room, Riley dreamed he was surrounded by polar bears. He fed them fish after fish, but still they growled for more.

At breakfast, Riley and Alice found Uncle Max talking to a wildlife management officer.

"These bears need food," said Uncle Max.

"I agree," the officer replied. "Normally, polar bears spend November to June hunting seals from the ice so they can store up enough fat to survive the warmer months. The rest of the year, they live on the shore and eat almost nothing. No ice means no food."

**Ringed Seal**

➤ It is the polar bear's main prey.

➤ It is the smallest of the arctic seals, with a maximum weight of 240 lbs. (108 kg).

➤ A mother ringed seal gives birth to babies in a special cave in the ice and snow called a "birthing lair," which protects her from bad weather and polar bears.

—Charles W. Potter, Collections Manager, Marine Mammals, National Museum of Natural History, Smithsonian Institution

"I think that's our main problem here," said Uncle Max. "Research shows that the Arctic has been getting warmer than normal in recent years, causing Hudson Bay to freeze later and later. For every week the bay doesn't freeze, adult bears lose about twenty-two pounds. And when the females don't get enough to eat, they give birth to fewer cubs, and aren't able to nurse the cubs they have."

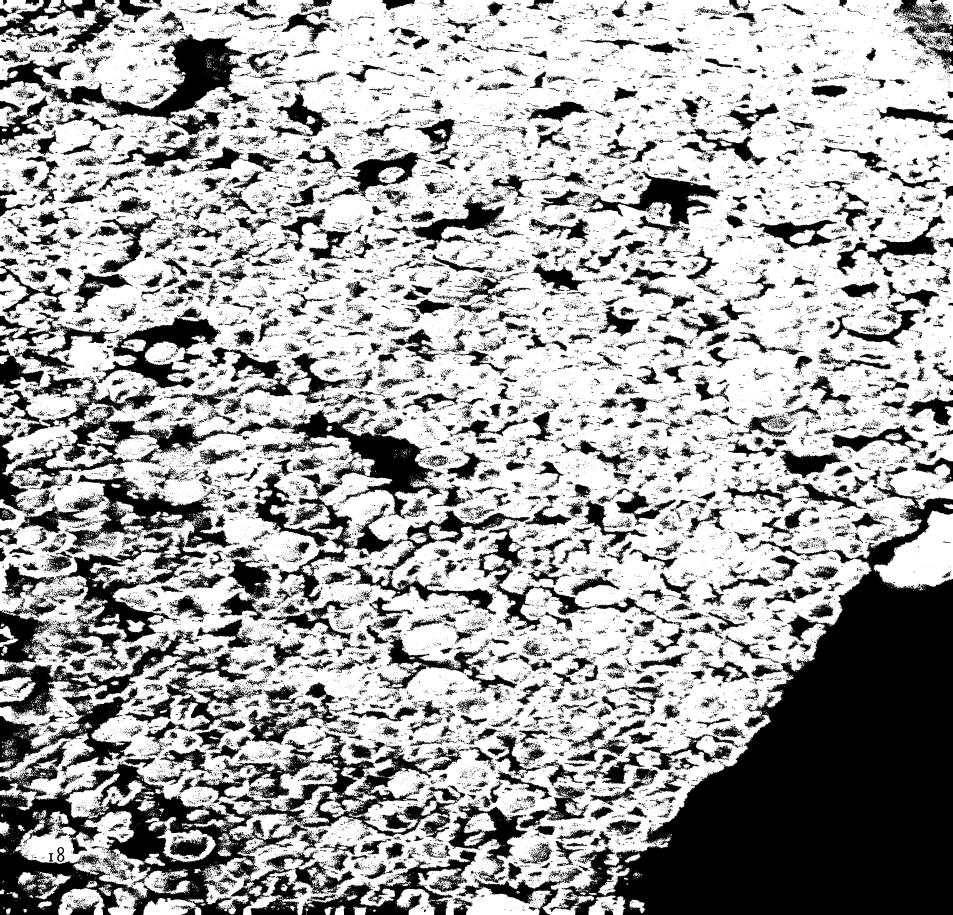

18

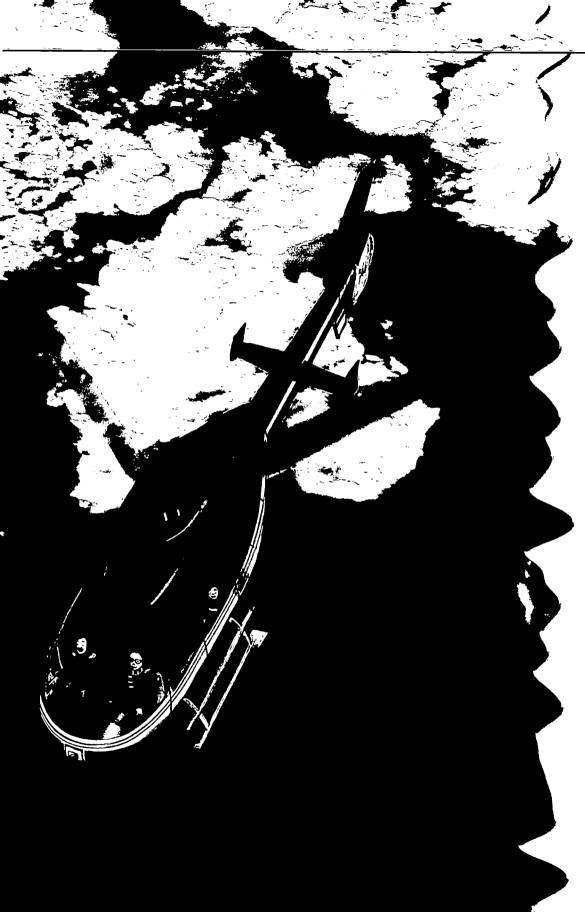

Later that day, Aunt Martha took them on a helicopter tour of Hudson Bay.

"The ice looks like a jigsaw puzzle with a million unconnected pieces," said Riley.

"That's because temperatures have stayed below freezing today," said Uncle Max. "Let's hope this is the beginning of the solid ice pack. In the last twenty years, the Hudson Bay polar bear population has dropped from 1,200 bears to 950 bears. If their hunting season keeps getting shorter because of the warming **climate**, polar bears in the wild could disappear within one hundred years."

A well-fed bear is a happy bear, remembered Riley.

"I have an idea," he told Alice.

That evening, Riley and Alice took their leftovers outside. Riley set the napkin of food on the ground and opened it.

*GROWWWWL!*

It was a POLAR BEAR! Alice screamed. Riley grabbed her hand, and they dashed into their room.

"Maybe feeding the bears wasn't such a good idea after all," said Alice, still shaking.

Riley and Alice were too scared to sleep. They stayed up all night, watching out for polar bears. Suddenly, something banged on their door and burst inside! Riley jumped out of bed, while Alice jumped farther in.

Whew! It was just Uncle Max.

"The polar bear jail is overflowing!" Uncle Max cried. "Aunt Martha is making an emergency bear drop, and we need your help!"

At the jail, they saw a polar bear wrapped in a cargo net.

"There are too many bears looking for food in town," said the wildlife officer. "Someone left food out for this one last night."

"That was us," said Riley, turning red. "We thought we were helping."

"Feeding bears is VERY dangerous, and teaching them to rely on humans won't solve their problems," said Uncle Max. "Here comes Aunt Martha now."

"We're sorry," Alice said. "Will the bear be okay?"

"I hope so," said Uncle Max.

23

24

## Caribou

➤ While North Americans call it a caribou, the rest of the world calls it a reindeer!

➤ It regularly digs down through the snow (cratering) to find its favorite food, a lichen known as "reindeer moss."

➤ Both the male and female caribou grow antlers.

—Joel Berger,
Senior Scientist, Wildlife
Conservation Society

As they flew over the tundra, they watched a herd of caribou through the snowy mist.

# Polar Bear

➤ It isn't white! Its skin is black and its hair is actually free of **pigment**. Its fur just appears white when it's clean and in the sunlight.

➤ The North Pole region is the only place to find a polar bear—you won't find one at the South Pole!

➤ While stalking a seal, a polar bear will place each paw softly on the snow to keep from scaring away its prey with a crunch.

—Robert Buchanan, President, Polar Bears International

"Look! The bay has frozen over! I can see bears walking on it!" said Riley.
"Just in time," said Uncle Max.

Aunt Martha landed near the edge of the bay. Everyone jumped into action. Riley and Alice watched for other polar bears, while Aunt Martha unhooked the net and Uncle Max loosened the straps. The bear began to stir.

"We have to free him quickly!" said Uncle Max.

"The net is stuck on his ear!" Alice cried.

"It's also caught on his back paw!" shouted Riley.

"Careful!" warned Uncle Max. Riley's heart was pounding as he lifted the net over the bear's sharp claws. The bear growled softly just as Riley got him loose.

"Great job, Carrot Top!" said Uncle Max. "Now let's go!"

As the helicopter lifted off, they watched the bear stand up and move slowly onto the newly frozen seawater.

"We did it!" said Alice.

"Hopefully this bear will be eating seal for supper," said Aunt Martha.

"You guys were great," said Uncle Max. "Thankfully, the ice froze today, and the bears will survive another year. But **climate** change is still a big problem for polar bears, and with temperatures rising twice as fast in the Arctic as in the rest of the world, they are still at great risk."